A Chip Off the Old Block

JODY JENSEN SHAFFER

ILLUSTRATED BY DANIEL MIYARES

NANCY PAULSEN BOOKS

AUNT ETNA

UNCLE GIBRALTAR

MOM AND DAD

GREAT-GRANDMA
HALF DOME

Rocky was part of a great big family.

MY COUSINS

THE WAVE

DINO

THE TOWER

RUSHMORE

Tons of his relatives were rock stars!

He loved when his parents told him about
the most remarkable ones.
Uncle Gibraltar ruled over massive ships
and huge oceans.

Aunt Etna could put on a
light show like no one else.

And Great-Grandma Half Dome
lived just a stone's throw away.

"I want to do something important, too!"
said Rocky.
"But you're just a pebble," said his mom.
"A chip off the old block," said his dad.

But inside, Rocky was a boulder! He was
little, but he knew he could do big things.
That night, after his parents went to bed,
Rocky made his plan. "I'll join my cousin and
become part of one of the most amazing
formations on Earth!"

The next morning, Rocky hopped a ride to Arizona.

He landed with a

THUNK.

Rocky was just settling in with his cousin
The Wave when a strong wind whisked him
away. "Whoa!"

"Dude!" shouted his cousin. "Way to catch
some air!"

Rocky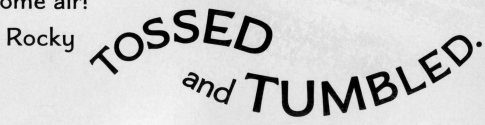

And when he landed, he noticed a piece of him had broken off. "Oh, no! I hope I'm still big enough to make a difference."

Rocky was smaller, but he remembered another relative who stood tall.

So he caught a ride to Wyoming!

Rocky landed with a *THUD.*

He had almost anchored
himself to his towering cousin
when a storm rolled in and
washed him away.

WHOOSH!

"Help!" Rocky gurgled.
"Enjoy the ride, Rocky!"
his cousin yelled back.
(It was clear the two of them
didn't share the same sediment.)

Rocky swooped and bounced until he hit a tree . . .

THWACK!

. . . and landed
on a car.

But he wasn't giving up.

"I know I can still matter," he said.
"I can be big with my cousins in Texas!"

After a long trip south, Rocky landed with a **PLOP.**

"I'll safeguard these ancient sauropod tracks!" he said.

Rocky was doing a great job until an armadillo sent him skipping.

"Yiiiiikes!"

Rocky was disappointed, but he was still ready to roll. He set his sights on South Dakota.

Rocky bumped and bounced all the way to Mount Rushmore.

He landed with a *PLONK*.
"I may be tiny, but I can still rock a souvenir stand!"

EL COME!

PINS   1/2 off

He was surveying his surroundings when he overheard a worker. "Sorry, folks. Park's closed. Lincoln's nose is cracked!"

Rocky was crushed. He had traveled so far, searched so hard, lost so much mass. "Now I'll never be great like my relatives."

Then he looked up. Something about that majestic mountain reminded him what he was made of. "Cousin Rushmore may be monumental. But everybody needs a little help sometimes!"

Rocky hitched a
ride to the top,

climbed out for a better look . . .

. . . and jumped.

"ROCK

AND ROLLLLLLL!"

Rocky dove over Lincoln's hair,
somersaulted past Lincoln's forehead,
surfed between Lincoln's eyebrows,
and landed . . .

PLINK!

. . . in the crack in Lincoln's nose.
He was a perfect fit!
  "I did it! I did something important!
I saved Abraham Lincoln!"
  "Solid!" said his cousin.

Workers hugged, reporters snapped pictures, and Mount Rushmore opened as usual.

All thanks to Rocky, the little pebble that wouldn't be taken for granite.

A Few Words About Rock Types

IGNEOUS: Igneous rocks are formed from cooled magma. Magma is heated and liquefied rock from below Earth's crust. When magma erupts in a volcano, it becomes lava, a type of igneous rock. Granite, basalt, and pumice are igneous rocks.

METAMORPHIC: Any rock that changes can become a metamorphic rock. Rocks that are moved to new places and become unstable or those exposed to high temperatures and lots of pressure can become metamorphic. Slate, schist, gneiss, and marble are metamorphic rocks.

SEDIMENTARY: Sedimentary rocks cover the earth. They are made from pieces of other rocks that have settled, accumulated, and become compacted. Sandstone, limestone, shale, and coal are sedimentary.

Rocky's Rock Star Family

ROCKY
A little pebble with boulder-sized dreams.
Type: sedimentary

ROCKY'S MOM
No matter how important her son becomes, he'll always be her little pebble.
Type: sedimentary

ROCKY'S DAD
Happy to sit at home and gather moss.
Type: sedimentary

THE ROCK OF GIBRALTAR—Iberian Peninsula, Gibraltar
Rocky's uncle and the patriarch of the family.
Type: sedimentary; made of limestone
Outstanding trait: At 1,396 feet, he watches over ship traffic from the Atlantic Ocean and the Mediterranean Sea through the Strait of Gibraltar.

MOUNT ETNA—Sicily, Italy
Rocky's aunt. She can really light up the night.
Type: igneous; made of hardened lava, volcanic ash, and pumice
Outstanding trait: Nearly 11,000 feet tall, she regularly spews molten lava into the air. This Italian powerhouse has the longest written record of volcanic eruptions in history.

HALF DOME—California
Rocky's great-grandma.
Type: igneous; made of granite
Outstanding trait: Rising above her surroundings in Yosemite National Park, this great-grandma has one sheer side, making her look like she's only half there!

THE WAVE—Arizona
Rocky's cool cousin.
Type: sedimentary; made of sandstone
Outstanding trait: The Wave is made of fiery swirls of bright orange, pink, yellow, and red. Sculpted by years of rain and wind, it seems to change colors, dude.

DEVILS TOWER, aka BEAR LODGE—Wyoming
Rocky's looming cousin.
Type: igneous; made of cooled magma
Outstanding trait: Sporting a mean flattop and rising high above the landscape, Devils Tower is made up of striking vertical columns.

DINOSAUR VALLEY—Texas
Rocky's dino-loving cousins.
Type: sedimentary; made of limestone, sandstone, mudstone
Outstanding trait: Millions of years ago, dinosaurs tromped in Texas! Their footprints were found preserved in the limestone banks of the Paluxy River, proving that sauropods walked on land.

MOUNT RUSHMORE—South Dakota
Rocky's monumental cousin, also known as the Shrine of Democracy.
Type: igneous; made of granite
Outstanding trait: Carved from a granite mountainside, Mount Rushmore features the faces of U.S. presidents George Washington, Thomas Jefferson, Theodore Roosevelt, and Abraham Lincoln.

AUTHOR'S NOTE

The faces on Mount Rushmore actually *do* crack from time to time! Mount Rushmore's sculptor, Gutzon Borglum, originally created a sealant of linseed oil, white lead, and granite dust. But his sealant dried out quickly and let water seep in. The National Park Service now uses a silicone sealant, camouflaged with granite dust, to fix cracks. They also installed an electronic monitoring system to detect new ones.

To all my rock star relatives, with love —J.J.S.

For Stella and Sam, my two chips off the old block —D.M.

Nancy Paulsen Books
an imprint of Penguin Random House LLC
375 Hudson Street
New York, NY 10014

Library of Congress Cataloging-in-Publication Data
Names: Shaffer, Jody Jensen, author. | Miyares, Daniel, illustrator.
Title: A chip off the old block / Jody Jensen Shaffer ; illustrated by Daniel Miyares.
Description: New York, NY : Nancy Paulsen Books, [2018]
Summary: Rocky, only a pebble, is determined to be as great as his famous relatives, so he travels from one family member
to another until he finds the spot where he can make a big difference. Includes facts about types of rocks, the famous rocks
mentioned, and Mount Rushmore.
Identifiers: LCCN 2017009140 | ISBN 9780399173882
Subjects: | CYAC: Rocks—Fiction. | Voyages and travels—Fiction. | National monuments--Fiction.
Classification: LCC PZ7.1.S4745 Chi 2018 | DDC [E]—dc23
LC record available at https://lccn.loc.gov/2017009140

Printed in the U.S.A. by Phoenix Color, Hagerstown, MD.
ISBN 9780399173882
3 5 7 9 10 8 6 4 2

Design by Eileen Savage.
Text set in Boucherie Flared, Boucherie Sans and Neutraface Text.
The art for this book was made by using watercolor and acrylic paints on paper, as well as digital tools.